For my Spider,
forever brave and
true to yourself
— E.J.

The illustrations in this book were drawn by hand using traditional and digital methods

First published in Swedish as *Superhjälte Prinsessan* by Rabén & Sjögren, Stockholm in 2022
First published in English by Floris Books, Edinburgh in 2024. Swedish text © 2022 Emily Joof
English text © 2024 Emily Joof. Illustrations © 2022 Åsa Gilland. Author photo © Lena Nian. Illustrator
photo © Åsa Gilland. All rights reserved. No part of this publication may be reproduced without the
prior permission of Floris Books, Edinburgh www.florisbooks.co.uk British Library CIP data available
ISBN 978-178250-884-7 Printed in China by Leo Paper Products Ltd

FSC
www.fsc.org
MIX
Paper | Supporting
responsible forestry
FSC® C020056

Printed on sustainably
sourced FSC® certified
paper. Uses plant-based
inks which reduce
chemical emissions.

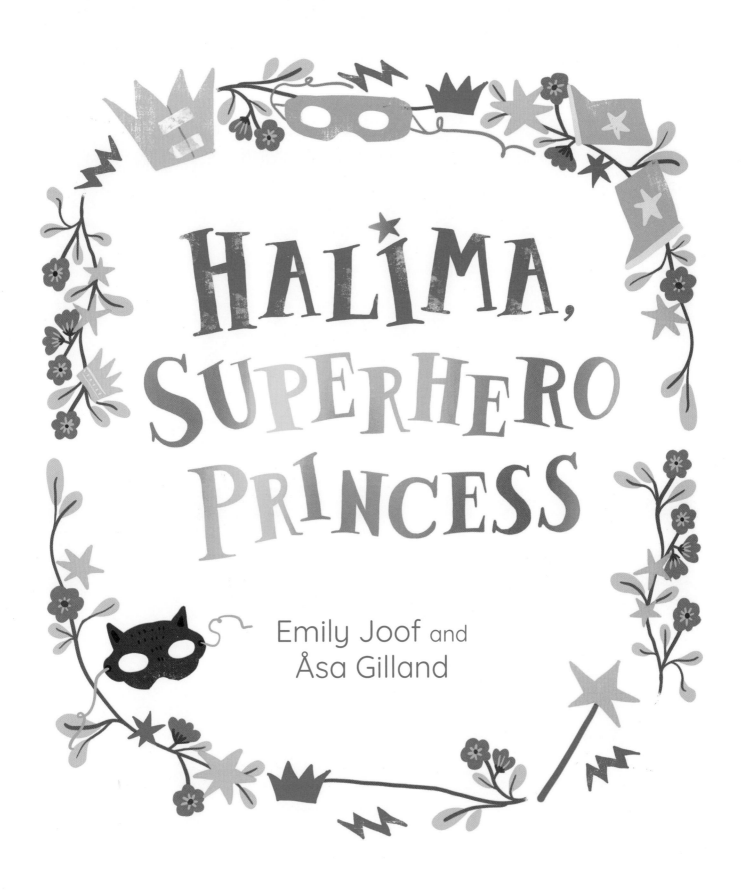

HALIMA, SUPERHERO PRINCESS

Emily Joof and
Åsa Gilland

Floris
Books

Astrid and Maya are my best friends in the whole wide world. We share ALL our secrets. We love eating cucumber, making slime, and being pirates and space explorers.

One day, our friend Alexis invited us all to her sixth birthday party – a superhero and princess party!

We had an emergency meeting.

"I'm going as Iron Man!" Maya grinned, showing the gap between her front teeth. "We have lots of old boxes to make a cool costume... Or I could be Cinderella, with my outfit from Halloween."

"I'm going as a princess!" said Astrid excitedly. "I have all the costumes – Rapunzel, Snow White, Anna and Elsa. I can't wait!"

"I want to be Elsa too," I said. "Or Pippi Longstocking. She's sort of a superhero. She helps children when they don't have any money to buy candy. She's the best!"

"But, Halima..." Maya said, looking puzzled, "you can't be Pippi or Elsa, even with a costume. How would you look like them?"

"Maybe with a mask and a wig?" Astrid offered, trying to be kind.

I felt a big grey cloud fill my tummy, and
suddenly it was too cold to be outside. It took
all my energy to carry the grey cloud inside me.
I spent the rest of the day feeling very small.

"How exciting, Halima!" said Mama, when she saw the party invitation. "Who do you want to go as?"

"I don't want to go," I mumbled.

"Why not?" she asked. "You love parties and dressing up. You are totally a superhero or a princess every day! What's wrong?"

"I want to go to the party as someone strong and brave," I told her. "But I can't be a superhero princess like Elsa or Pippi because I don't look like them or have the right hair. Are there any cool people who look more like me, Mama?"

"Oh, come here, Halima," she said gently. "First of all,
if you want to be Elsa or Pippi, you can definitely be
Elsa or Pippi. In fact, you would make the best and the
boldest Elsa or Pippi in the whole entire world!"

"Secondly, your hair has superpowers. It is MAGICAL!
No other kind of hair can do what yours can."

AFRO PUFFS

LOCS

FAUXHAWK

PRESSED STRAIGHT

BRAIDS

"And finally," Mama carried on proudly, "there are
LOTS of brave, strong, cool, clever people who look
more like you all over the world..."

"There's Serena, Kadeena,
Simone and Misty,

Meghan, Maya, Ellen and Michelle,

Janelle, Willow, Nikeisha and Beyoncé,

Yara, Lupita and Kamala,

Amanda, Tess, Mae and Malala,

and don't forget Kamala, Shuri, Storm and Monica!"

"These incredible women sparkle and shine," Mama continued. "They are brave, they are smart and they stand up for others. And that, Halima, is what makes a superhero princess."

"Maybe I could go to the party as one of them?" I said.

"Let's try out some costumes together this week," Mama suggested. "How does that sound?"

"It sounds like a plan!"
I said, running to my
craft cupboard.

MONDAY

Storm – commander
of the weather and
star of the X-Men!

TUESDAY

Mae Jemison –
space explorer
and adventurer
of the galaxy!

WEDNESDAY

Janelle Monáe – guitar-genius
pop star and amazing actor!

THURSDAY

Misty Copeland
– inspirational
twirl goddess and
ballerina princess!

FRIDAY

Shuri – awesome
princess of Wakanda
and inventor of
spy gadgets!

SATURDAY was hair-washing day and the day of the party.
Mama and I munched some berries while we waited for
the deep conditioner to work through my hair.

"So, have you decided who you're going to dress up as?" Mama asked.

"Yup... you'll see," I replied. "I'll need a fauxhawk to match my outfit, though. Can we do that?"

"One fauxhawk, coming right up!" Mama grinned.

Then I ran into my room to get changed.

SILVER SPACE BOOTS ✓
YELLOW BATHING SUIT ✓
CUT-OUT 'H' TO STICK ON ✓
RAINBOW LEGGINGS ✓
GLITTER CAPE ✓
INVENTOR GOGGLES ✓
TIARA ✓

The doorbell rang.
"Halima! Astrid and Maya are here.
Are you ready?" Mama called.

I burst out of my room and flew towards them.

"Wow, Halima, you look AMAZING!" said Maya.

"What costume IS that?!" asked Astrid.

"I'm Halima, Superhero Princess!" I declared. "The world is ready for a new superhero. Let's go!"

MEET MAMA'S INCREDIBLE WOMEN AND GIRLS!

AMANDA GORMAN
Poet and activist

BEYONCÉ
Singer

ELLEN JOHNSON SIRLEAF
Former President of
Liberia and Nobel
Peace Prize winner

JANELLE MONÁE
Singer and actor

KADEENA COX
Para athlete

KAMALA HARRIS
Vice President
of the USA

KAMALA KHAN
Superhero

LUPITA NYONG'O
Actor

MAE JEMISON
Scientist and
astronaut

MALALA YOUSAFZAI
Human rights activist

MAYA ANGELOU
Author and
human rights activist

MEGHAN MARKLE
Actor and
Duchess of Sussex

MICHELLE OBAMA
Lawyer, author and
former First Lady
of the USA

MISTY COPELAND
Ballet dancer

MONICA RAMBEAU
Superhero

NIKEISHA ANDERSSON
Music video producer

SERENA WILLIAMS
Tennis player

SHURI
Superhero

SIMONE BILES
Gymnast

STORM
Superhero

TESS ASPLUND
Anti-racism activist

WILLOW SMITH
Singer and actor

YARA SHAHIDI
Actor

ME!
Superhero princess